LITTLE WORM'S BIG QUESTION

Schlunke & Polyp

For Issa and Mariama

Once upon a time there was a little worm,
who lived in a dark, damp hole in the ground.

All he ever had to eat was mud.

He had mud for
breakfast, mud for
lunch, and mud
for dinner.

He was not
a very happy
little worm.

One morning he got up extra early to have a nice crawl in the fresh air, and to get away from all that mud...

...but the crows were waiting for him.

Luckily, the sound of footsteps scared them off,
and just as Little Worm thought it
was safe to wriggle on his way...

SPLAT!

He got
trodden on
by a boot!

A great big *muddy* boot!

Well, that was it. He'd had enough.

He'd been bullied, squashed, and now he was all covered in mud!

He was so unhappy that he burst into tears.

A passing grasshopper heard him crying,
and jumped over to ask what was wrong.

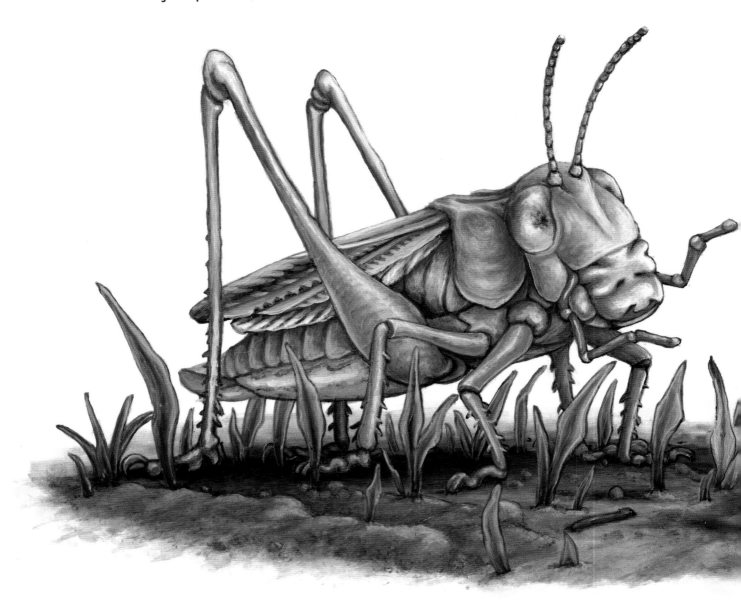

'Nobody respects me!' wailed Little Worm.
'Everyone looks down on me!
I'm nothing but a worthless little worm.'

'No you're not!' exclaimed the
grasshopper. 'No-one is worthless!

'Look at me – I'm not much bigger
than you, and I get picked on as well.
But I can jump 20 times my own height.
That makes me very special.

'There's something special about
everyone – including you.

'You just need to
find out what it is.'

And before Little Worm could
reply, the grasshopper leapt
into the air and was gone.

It was true. She really
could jump 20 times
her own height.

This left
Little Worm
with a big question –
what on earth could
be special about him?

Although he couldn't
think of anything, he was
determined to find out.

And that's when he had an idea.

He decided he would travel all the way
around the world and ask every animal he met
what it was that made *them* special.

Maybe that way he'd find
the answer to his big question.

So he went home, packed his rucksack, and set out on his journey.

He hadn't travelled far when he came across a
pompous peacock, parading up and down in a field.

'Excuse me, Mr Peacock,' said Little Worm.
'What is it about you that makes you special?'

'Well isn't it *obvious*?' sneered the peacock. 'Look at
my gorgeous feathers! Can't you see this magnificent tail?
Why, I'm the most beautiful bird in the world! Everyone says so.
That's what makes *me* special.'

And it was true. He really was an impressive sight.

Little Worm knew that he didn't have any beautiful
feathers – he didn't have any feathers at all. So that
couldn't be what was special about him.

And, with a sigh, he continued on his way.

In the middle of a hot, dry desert, he came upon
a captivating cobra, curling across the sand.

'Good day to you, Ms Cobra,' said Little Worm.
'What is it about you that makes you special?'

'Nobody crosses my path,' hissed the cobra, 'and do you know why?
Because I'm the most venomous snake to slither these sands.
I can kill with one bite. I'm feared and respected.
That's what makes *me* special.'

And it was true. She really did look very frightening.

Little Worm knew for sure that no-one was afraid of him.
He couldn't hurt anyone, even if he wanted to.
That couldn't be what made him special.

So he took a big gulp of water from his flask
and continued on his way.

Heading north – as far north as you can go – he found
a ponderous polar bear, posing on an iceberg.

'Sorry to interrupt, Mr Polar Bear,' said Little Worm.
'What is it about you that makes you special?'

'That's a deep question, brother,' rumbled the polar bear.
'You could say I'm the coolest bear in this frozen neighborhood –
I'm chilled out because I'm so *warm*.
Check these furs and this nice thick layer of bear fat.
Fact is, I'm an *insulated* kind of guy. That's what makes
me special, my wriggly little friend... *yeah*.'

And it was true – he did look very relaxed and cozy.

Little Worm knew he wasn't very well insulated.
In fact, he was so cold right now, he couldn't even feel his own tail.
He knew that keeping warm wasn't what made him special.

So, with his teeth chattering, he continued on his way.

Hacking his way through the jungle, he caught sight of
a boastful beetle, balancing on top of a fallen tree.

'I don't mean to bother you, Mr Beetle,' said Little Worm,
 'but what is it about you that makes you special?'

'You want to know what makes me special?!' shouted the beetle.
'I'm lifting 85 times my own body weight here, pal! No-one can
beat that! I'm the strongest – that's what makes *me* special!'

And it was true. He really was very powerful
to be able to lift something *that* heavy.

Little Worm knew he was no weightlifter.
It was a real effort for him just to lift his own nose off the ground.
So he was pretty sure it wasn't strength that made him special.

He left the beetle to his showing off
and continued on his way.

Paddling across the ocean, he saw a
wondrous whale, whooshing out of the waves.

'Ahoy there, Ms Whale!' yelled Little Worm. 'You're an amazing sight.
What is it about you that makes you special?'

'My enormous size, landlubber!' boomed the whale.
'I am without a doubt the biggest creature ever to have
lived on this earth. That's what makes *me* special!'

And it was true. The splash she made as
she hit the water was truly spectacular.

Little Worm knew that, compared to her, he was tiny.
He was, after all, a *little* worm, so that definitely wasn't
what made him special.

With a half-hearted 'Yo ho ho', he continued on his way.

He took to the air, and crossed the path of a
formidable falcon, flying through the clouds.

'I say, old girl,' hollered Little Worm, 'be a sport and let me in
on a secret... what is it about you that makes you special?'

'Ha! That's easy!' announced the falcon.
'I'm the fastest animal on the planet!

'Watch this!'

Down she dived, and it was true – she was gone in a flash!

Little Worm knew he wasn't that fast. In fact, his top
speed was only a slow wriggle. There was no way that
being quick was what made him special.

So he landed, and feeling a bit wobbly,
he continued on his way.

Diving under the sea, he spotted an
outrageous octopus, occupying a rock.

'Can you please tell me, Mr Octopus,' pleaded Little Worm,
'what is it about you that makes you special?'

'I'm glad you asked me that,' bubbled the octopus,
'because you'd never guess. Are you ready?

Don't blink, now... One... Two... Three...'

And he vanished!

'Did you see that?' said a voice from nowhere. 'I'm the master
of disguise. I can change my shape and color any time I want!
It's called *camouflage*. That's what makes *me* special!'

And it was true. He now looked so much like the rock
he'd been sitting on that he was completely invisible.

Little Worm knew that he wasn't able to disguise himself...
he couldn't even make himself look like a *stick*.
That couldn't be what made him special.

So he rose to the surface and continued on his way.

He took a giant leap for wormkind and hitched a ride to the moon.

He soon found himself face to face with an
awkward astronaut, approaching across the dusty plains.

'BEEP! Are you receiving me, Mr Human?' asked Little Worm.
'What is it about you that makes you special? Over.'

'Copy you, Little Worm,' crackled the astronaut.
'Humans are the smartest animal in the world.
Our big brains mean we can do almost anything we want.

'But, seeing the fragile Earth hanging there in space,
I can't help wondering if we really are that clever, or just plain dumb.
It's our only home, and we treat it real bad.'

'Copy that.' replied Little Worm. 'BEEP!'

Little Worm knew he wasn't very smart.
If he was, he would have already worked out what made him special.
But he *still* didn't know the answer.

And so, with nowhere left to go,
he began the long journey home.

When he arrived back at his dark, damp hole
in the ground, his heart sank. Maybe there wasn't
anything special about him, and he really *was*
just a worthless little worm.

But then, through the rain,
a voice called out to him:
'What's the matter with you then?'

And, when he looked up, he saw it was *another* little worm.

Little Worm told her his story: all the strange
places he'd been, all the different animals he'd met,
the big question he'd asked, and how he'd failed to find an answer.

'Don't be daft!' she exclaimed. 'You're dead brave to have
gone on a huge journey like that, but the answer's simple!
It's been right here all along...

'You're a worm!

'Never mind that lot with their fancy feathers and moon walks –
it's us worms who are the most important creatures in the world!

'All that stuff we eat – it goes in one end as mud and compost and bits of old leaves, and comes out the other as rich and healthy soil.

'When we all burrow through the ground together,
it lets in the air and water that the plants need.

'If it weren't for us, nothing would grow, and the other animals wouldn't have anything to eat, would they?

That's what makes you special...
It's what makes all of us little worms special!

'So just you remember that – be proud of what you are!'

'And who knows', she said
as she wiggled away...

'Maybe I'll see you
around some time?'

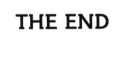

THE END

The tail feathers of the **male peacock** are prized as decorative items, and have been farmed for thousands of years. They molt naturally every year, but some farms pluck them from the birds. The vivid colors of the 'eyes' are an optical illusion created by tiny crystal-like structures within the feathers that diffract the light.

The venom in a single **Egyptian cobra** bite can kill an elephant, or 20 human beings. Despite this, the Egyptian mongoose is known regularly to hunt and eat the snakes, and has a high level of resistance to their toxic bites.

Polar bears are so well insulated against the cold that they are almost invisible to infra-red scans. The melting of the polar ice caps caused by global warming threatens their natural habitat and food supply, and so their numbers are in decline. Spills from oil or gas drilling pollute their fur, and stop it from keeping them warm.

The **hercules beetle** lives in the rainforests of Central and South America. Its jaws can lift 85 times its own body weight: the same as a human being able to lift six metric tons, which is about the weight of four cars. In the past 50 years, 17 per cent of the Amazon rainforest has been destroyed by logging, most of it to create pasture for cattle.

Around 30 meters long and weighing 180 metric tons, the **blue whale** is the largest animal that has ever existed. They were hunted almost to extinction by humans until this was banned in the 1970s. Although still an endangered species, blue whale numbers are now slowly beginning to recover.

Able to dive through the air at speeds of over 350 kilometers an hour, **peregrine falcons** are the fastest animals in existence, and have been kept in captivity for thousands of years by humans wanting to use them for hunting.

Octopuses have an astonishing ability to camouflage themselves rapidly. Small sacs of color on their surface stretch out to match the colors of their surroundings, and they can alter the texture of their skin, making themselves almost completely invisible. Like many species, they and their habitats are endangered by the use of huge fishing nets that trawl the sea bed.

'It's lonely. It's small. It's isolated, and there is no resupply. And we are mistreating it. Clearly, the highest loyalty we should have is not to our own country or our own religion or our hometown or even to ourselves. It should be to… the planet at large. This is our home, and this is all we've got.'
Astronaut Scott Carpenter

Lots more at:
littleworm.org

Photo credits: [peacock feather] Michael Maggs/Creative Commons; [mongoose] גיזונים/Creative Commons; [oil rig] Olav Gjerstad/Creative Commons; [logs] Dtfoxfoto/ Dreamstime.com/ Mill Ops Photo; [harpoon cannon] Rama/Creative Commons; [harpoon sea background] Shannon Rankin/NOAA; [falcon] Tilo Hauke/Creative Commons; [fishing net] Bo Pardau, flickr.com/photos/bodiver; [Earth] NASA.

Little Worm's Big Question
First published in 2016 by
New Internationalist Publications Ltd
The Old Music Hall
106-108 Cowley Road
Oxford OX4 1JE, UK
newint.org

Authors' acknowledgements
With many thanks to: Dr Dmitri Luganov, curator of arthropods, Manchester Museum; Dr Franciska De Vries, BBSRC
David Phillips Fellow, Faculty of Life Sciences, University of Manchester; Bo Pardau, photographer, flickr.com/photos/
bodiver; Ethical Consumer Magazine; and all our friends who offered so many great ideas and so much good advice.

Printed by 1010 Printing International Limited, Hong Kong, who hold environmental accreditation ISO 14001.

British Library Cataloguing-in-Publication Data
A catalogue record for this book is available from the British Library.

Library of Congress Cataloging-in-Publication Data
A catalog record for this book is available from the Library of Congress.

ISBN: 978-1-78026-261-1